M000085401

Strider

A PLAY WITH MUSIC

by

MARK ROZOVSKY

Apated from a Story by

Leo Tolstoy

English Stage Version by

ROBERT KALFIN & STEVE BROWN

Based on a Translation by

TAMARA BERING SUNGUROFF

Music Originally Composed by

MARK ROZOVSKY, S. VETIN

Original Russian Lyrics by

URI RIASHENTSEV

Adaptor, Composer of New Additional Music

NORMAN L. BERMAN

New English Lyrics by

STEVE BROWN

A SAMUEL FRENCH ACTING EDITION

SAMUEL FRENCH

FOUNDED 1830

New York   Hollywood   London   Toronto

SAMUELFRENCH.COM

IMPORTANT ADVERTISING NOTE

ALL producers of STRIDER shall announce the names of Mark Rozovsky, S. Vetkin and Uri Rıashentsev as original authors/composers of the work and the names of Robert Kalfin, Steve Brown, and Norman L. Berman as adaptors of the English-language version of the work on all programs, posters, and other paid advertısıng matter under the producers' control. The credıt to the authors/composers shall be not less than fifty percent (50%) of the size of type used for the tıtle of the work. Saıd bıllıng shall appear on separate lines followıng the tıtle of the work and shall be in the followıng form:

(Name of Producer)

presents

STRIDER

A Play with Music by
MARK ROZOVSKY

Adapted from a Story by
Leo Tolstoy

English Stage Version by
ROBERT KALFIN & STEVE BROWN

Based on a Translation by
TAMARA BERING SUNGUROFF

Music Originally Composed by	*Original Russian Lyrics by*
MARK ROZOVSKY, S. VETKIN	**URI RIASHENTSEV**

Adaptor, Composer of New Addıtıonal Music
NORMAN L. BERMAN

New English Lyrics by
STEVE BROWN

THE CHELSEA THEATER CENTER PRODUCTION
Originally produced on Broadway by **ARTHUR WHITELAW**
and **MIRIAM BIENSTOCK** *in association with* **LITA STARR**

HELEN HAYES THEATRE
OPERATED BY LESTER OSTERMAN

ARTHUR WHITELAW *and* **MIRIAM BIENSTOCK**
in association with **LITA STARR**
present
The Chelsea Theatre Production of

GERALD HIKEN
in

STRIDER ·

A Play with Music by
MARK ROZOVSKY

Adapted from a Story by
LEO TOLSTOY

also starring

GORDON	PAMELA	BENJAMIN
GOULD	BURRELL	HENDRICKSON

ROGER DeKOVEN   IGORS GAVON   RONNIE NEWMAN   SKIP LAWING

English Stage Version by
ROBERT KALFIN & STEVE BROWN

Based on a Translation by
TAMARA BERING SUNGUROFF

Music Originally Composed by   *Original Russian Lyrics by*
M. ROZOVSKY, S. VETKIN   **URI RIASHENTSEV**

Adaptor, Composer of New Additional Music
Vocal and Instrumental Arrangements & Musical Director
NORMAN L. BERMAN

New English Lyrics by
STEVE BROWN

Production Design by   *Costume Designs by*   *Lighting Design by*
WOLFGANG ROTH   **ANDREW B. MARLAY**   **ROBBY MONK**

Production Stage Manager   *Sound Design by*
ZOYA WYETH   **GARY HARRIS**

Directed and Staged by
ROBERT KALFIN and LYNNE GANNAWAY

CAST OF CHARACTERS
(*in order of speaking*)

Vaska/Mr. Willingstone .... Roger DeKoven
Prince Serpuhofsky .... Gordon Gould
General/Announcer .... Ronnie Newman
Viazapurikha/Mathieu/Marie .... Pamela Burrell
Strider .... Gerald Hiken
Actor .... Katherine-Mary Brown
Actor .... Jeannine Khoutieff
Actor .... Vicki Van Grack
Groom .... Skip Lawing
Gypsy . ... Nina Dova
Count Bobrinsky/Darling/The Lieutenant ....
Benjamin Hendrickson
Feofan/Fritz .... Igors Gavon
Bet Taker .... Vincent A. Feraudo
Vendor .... Charles Walker
Actor .... John Brownlee
Actor .... Nancy Kawalek
Gypsy .... Karen Trott
Actor .... Tad Ingram
Gypsy .... Steven Blane

5

DIRECTOR'S NOTE

The production is deliberately sparse. The intention is for the audience to do most of the work, filling the stage with their imaginations.

The set consists of a plain white canvas backdrop, three sets of white legs on each side of the stage used for entrances (stalls, etc.), a post downstage right with a water barrel, and a grindstone downstage left. The orchestra sits downstage left as well, left of the grindstone.

The only other major scenic pieces consist of several lengths of long ropes that are used for the castration scene, a chair that is brought on for the horse-selling scenes of both acts, two small tables with props that are used in the PRINCE-toilette/ STRIDER-grooming scene in Act I, a small stool or table that the bet-taker stands on for the race track scene, and an oriental rug and pillows that are MATHIEU's boudoir.

When forming the PRINCE's carriage in both acts, the actors attach a long length of leather rope encircling them which attaches to STRIDER's harness, and which they step into. A variation of this is used for the troika scene at the end of Act I. Only, this time, instead of leather, the sleigh is formed by a long length of blue ribbon attached to a blue ribbon harness.

The actors are costumed in simple, rough, peasant-like shirts, leggings and leg-wrappings in colors that evoke the colors of horses.

All of the horse "miming" is derived from a basic undulating movement that is common to all animals, man included. The actor portrays the front of the horse using his body from the waist up as the horse's neck, with his arms becoming the horse's front legs when he rears up. Otherwise, the horse is conveyed by the actor's use of his legs as the hind part of the horse, and by a switchlike tail made from a stick with lengths of cloth attached. The latter is held in the actors' hands. It is laid down, picked up, or stuck in the actors' back pocket or behind them in the top of their pants. It is freely used as needed.

6

Strider

ACT ONE

A small gypsy orchestra plays the overture. Half-way through, the ACTORS *enter playing tambourines and clapping. They join in singing and dancing. As the overture ends, they all go to their places for the beginning of the play, while the actor who plays* STRIDER *enters and stands by a hitching post and water barrel Downstage Right. Simultaneously, the actor who plays* VASKA *enters and lies down on the other side of the stage near a grindstone. He is a strange, thin figure dressed in a dirt-spattered kaftan.*

VASKA. (*Sings.*)
OH JESUS—IT'S TIME TO TAKE OUT THE NAGS!
BECAUSE OF THIS DUMB ANIMAL IT SEEMS
I NEVER GET TO FINISH HALF MY DREAMS
OH JESUS—IT'S TIME TO TAKE OUT THE NAGS!
(VASKA *falls asleep again.*)
CHORUS/HERD. (*A* MALE ACTOR.) Higher and higher rose the light of the sky. (*Another* MALE ACTOR/SERPUHOVSKY.) Wider and wider spread the streak of the dawn. (*A* FEMALE ACTOR/VIAZAPURIKHA.) Whiter grew the pale silver of the dew.
STRIDER. The piebald gelding stood alone. (*Carrying a make-up towel over his shoulder,* STRIDER *puts on make-up that gives his face brown and black piebald spots as the* CHORUS *describes him.*)
CHORUS/HERD. (*Another* FEMALE ACTOR.) His big, bony head with its deep hollowed eyes, and a drooping black under-lip that had once been torn, hung heavy and low on his neck. (*A* THIRD FEMALE ACTOR.) A neck which was so lean that it bent, and seemed to be carved of wood.
VASKA. (*Sings.*)
THIS CRAZYQUILT—SHOULD I HARNESS HIM
TODAY?

7

HIS BETTER DAYS ARE BURIED IN THE PAST
WHEN YOU'RE OLD YOU SHOULD BE DIGNIFIED
   OR NASTY
BUT PIEBALD—HE MEANS TO BE BOTH AT ONCE!
(*VASKA falls asleep again.*)
CHORUS/HERD (SECOND MALE ACTOR.) His forelegs were
crooked, bowed at the knees. (THIRD MALE ACTOR) There
were swellings over both hoofs, and on one leg—where the
piebald spot reached half-way down—there was a lump behind
the knee as big as a fist. (FOURTH MALE ACTOR.) The hocks of
his hind legs and the tail were stained from a chronic bowel
disorder.
VASKA (*Sings.*)
THIS PIEBALD IS STRANGE IN OTHER WAYS—
HE'S DEEP—WITH SPECIAL FEELINGS FOR A
   BEAST
LOOK, THERE'S THE SUN—A RASPBERRY IN THE
   EAST
OH JESUS—IT'S TIME TO TAKE OUT THE NAGS!
(*He sleeps again.*)
STRIDER. Yet, in spite of the loathsome old age to which this
horse had come, anyone looking at him could not help thinking,
and an expert would have said so at once, that in his day this
must have been a remarkably fine horse.
CHORUS/HERD. (*In unison.*) A remarkably fine horse. (*The*
CHORUS *leaves* VASKA *remains sleeping. Crickets are heard.
The actor playing* STRIDER *remains. He is wearing a costume
that is worn and spotted brown and black like a piebald horse,
above the shoes up to his knees, the legs are wrapped in old
linen rags as worn by Russian soldiers The* ACTOR *places
around his neck a rope that is hitched to the post. Then he
gazes at his tail. He looks at it as if studying it. Then he switches
it back and forth, swatting himself with it several times, the way
people switch themselves in a steam bath, but he does it lazily.
The* ACTOR *then walks over to the barrel of water and bends
over to drink, flicking his tail Having noisily drunk his fill, he
begins to rub his back against the post.*)
STRIDER (*Scratching himself*) Something itches me terribly.
Something's itching me terribly. (*Scratches one leg against the
other, flicks his tail. A barn door is heard banging open. A
shaft of light streaks into the barn.* COUNT BOBRINSKY *enters*

singing a tune to himself. He goes to a horse—a member of the
CHORUS, *leads it out from a stall created by the legs of the set,
and begins to harness it. Other horses stand in some of the other
stalls.*)

BOBRINSKY. (*Sings.*)
OH NEVER HAVE I THIRSTED FOR LIFE SO MUCH
BUT NOW THE HOUR HAS COME
AND NOW I MUST DIE. . . .
(*Goes to* STRIDER *and notices his condition.*) Damn. Vaska!

STRIDER. It itches me terribly.

BOBRINSKY. (*As though he has heard a sound somewhere
else in the barn.*) What?

STRIDER. Itches. (VASKA *snores.*)

BOBRINSKY. Vaska! Are you asleep?

VASKA. (*Sleepily.*) Huh? What? No, I'm just . . .

BOBRINSKY. (*Indicating* STRIDER.) Look at him! (*Cracking
his whip.*) Look at him!

VASKA. (*Goes to* STRIDER *feels his stomach and looks into
his mouth.*) It's the mange, your Excellency. Let me sell him
to the Gypsies.

BOBRINSKY. The gypsies? What's the use? Cut his throat.

VASKA. Cut his throat, we'll do that.

BOBRINSKY. Only get it done today. (*He leaves, singing the
tune as he leads his horse off.*)

VASKA. Cut his throat. So that's how it is, eh? (*Swings at*
STRIDER. STRIDER *neighs.* VASKA *crosses toward the grindstone, stops and pulls a knife from his boot.*) Now you're going
to get it! (*He goes to the grindstone and begins to sharpen it.
The audience hears the natural unpleasant grating sound of the
knife sharpening.* STRIDER, *tied to the post, calmly and dispas-
sionately watches* VASKA. *He gives the impression that he does
not understand the proceedings, and therefore does not react at
all. He closes his tired eyes. It seems that he is sleeping—like
a horse—standing up. The music begins to play, blending the
sound of the leitmotif. The* CHORUS *enters. In the course of the
play, the actors are transformed into various characters, at the
same time acting collectively as the* NARRATOR. *Members of the*
HERD *are dressed approximately the same way as* STRIDER:
in peasant shirts and pants with leggings. But they differ from
STRIDER *in being young and energetic. They come together and,
on a chord, look toward the audience.*)

CHORUS/HERD. (*Singing a cappella.*)
OH MORTAL—LIFE IS OVER QUICKLY
IT MAY BE BETTER THAT YOU CANNOT
     COMPREHEND HOW VERY BRIEF THE SPAN—
     HOW QUICK THE PASSING
THIS ONE REMEMBERS HE'S A CHURCHMAN
THIS ONE A LAWYER CALLS HIMSELF
AND THIS ONE MAY BE RICH—OR TSAR!
YET EV'RYONE FORGETS HE'S MORTAL!

POOR PIEBALD—YOU THOUGHT THAT YOU WERE
     HAPPY
IT LASTED ONLY FOR A MOMENT IN YOUR
     MINDLESS STATE OF BLISS
TIL MANKIND TAUGHT YOU SORROW
YOUR WEARY EYES SPEAK ONLY SADNESS
YOUR SOUL'S ASLEEP
AND THOUGH WE'RE GRIEVING FOR YOUR LIFE,
YOU MUST REMEMBER WHAT YOU ARE
ONLY MORTAL!
(STRIDER *unhitches himself from the post and slowly exits. To a musical transition, the* CHORUS *gradually transform into horses before our eyes; the animals created through movement and individual mannerisms—tossing their heads, snorting, etc.* VIAZAPURIKHA, *an old mare who is the leader of the group, eventually rallys them with a whinny into a tightly moving, galloping* HERD. *During the following song, the* HERD *changes direction as they seem to gallop over a field.*)

SONG OF THE HERD

OVER MEADOW—OVER PASTURE
ROAMS THE HUNDRED-HEADED STALLION
WITH A HUNDRED MANES IN MOTION
AND HIS SWEAT PERFUMES THE SUMMER
THOUGH A HUNDRED HEADS ARE TOSSING
THEY ARE TOSSING ALL AS ONE
AND IT COULDN'T BE MORE NAT'RAL
IN THE LOGIC OF THE HERD

WE'RE THE HERD—THE HERD—THE HERD

HEY-HO
WE'RE THE HERD—THE HERD—THE HERD
HEY-HO

(STRIDER *enters. The* HERD *senses his presence and begins to taunt him.* STRIDER *remains passive, somewhat confused at their behavior.*)

FIRST MALE HORSE. (FEOFAN.) Hey you! Gelding!
SECOND MALE HORSE. He's strange!
FIRST FEMALE HORSE He's different!
THIRD MALE HORSE. He's not one of us—he's an outsider!
SECOND FEMALE HORSE. *We're* all related to Smetanka, the famous race horse!
THIRD FEMALE HORSE. Nobody knows where *he* came from!
FOURTH FEMALE HORSE. (*Laughing.*) They bought him at a fair—for eighty paper rubles!
FOURTH MALE HORSE. He's old!
FIFTH MALE HORSE. He's a gelding!
SIXTH MALE HORSE (SERPUHOVSKY.) He's a nobody!
SEVENTH MALE HORSE. (*The* GENERAL.) Hey, you! Ugly one!
FIRST MALE HORSE. Come on, fellows, kick him!
EIGHTH MALE HORSE. (*The* GROOM.) Not like that. Look how I do it! (*He does a handstand, kicking with his hind legs.*)
THE MALE HERD MEMBERS (*Chanting.*)
EV'RY MEMBER OF THE HERD BEHAVES EXACTLY
     LIKE HIS BROTHER
          (*Female horses join the males.*)
WHETHER NEIGHING, WHETHER PLAYING
EACH THE IMAGE OF THE OTHER
CHORUS/HERD.
AND IF ANYONE IS DIFF'RENT HE'LL BE KICKED
     FROM MORN TO NIGHT
THAT'S WHY HOOVES ARE FOUND ON HORSES
     IN THE LOGIC OF THE HERD

(*The* HERD *begins to toss* STRIDER *from one to another beating and kicking him.* STRIDER *does not kick back but only breathes harder.*)

WE'RE THE HERD—THE HERD—THE HERD
THE HERD HEY-HO
WE'RE THE HERD—THE HERD—THE HERD
THE HERD HEY-HO
WE'RE THE HERD—THE HERD—THE HERD
THE HERD HEY-HO
WE'RE THE HERD—THE HERD—THE HERD
THE HERD HEY-HO

(*The* OLD MARE, VIAZAPURIKHA, *enters just as the* HERD *have thrown* STRIDER *to the ground. Her whinny "freezes" them. As she goes toward* STRIDER, *they all back away. She approaches* STRIDER *and sniffs him.*)

VIAZAPURIKHA. Strider . . .

HERD. (*Echoing, some with surprise, some with derision.*) Strider!

VIAZAPURIKHA. Of course, it's Strider. He's come back. Don't you recognize me? Why should you, I'm an old mare now . . . Viazapurikha! (*Laughs.*) Remember? (*They rub their manes, one against the other and both laugh.*) You remember me now.

STRIDER. Yes. I was born here. I am the son of Amiable-the-First. Baba was my dam. My pedigree name is Muzhik-the-First. My nickname is Strider.

HERD. Strider?!

VIAZAPURIKHA. (*Delighted.*) The crowd called him that because of his long stride—a stride as long as an arm's length of cloth measure—the likes of which was not to be found in all Russia.

STRIDER. Yes. In all the world there's not a horse with better lineage than mine. I would never have told you this. Why should I? You would never have known me: even Viazapurikha didn't recognize me till just now.

VIAZAPURIKHA. Strider, you're so . . . different . . . And still I did recognize you! Oh my!

STRIDER. I should never have told you this. I have no need to be pitied by my own kind . . . you insisted upon it.

HERD. (*An older Male Horse*/SERPUHOVSKY.) There is a majestic old age . . . (*Another Male Horse/The* GENERAL.) There is a repulsive old age . . .

A FEMALE HORSE. There is a pitiful old age. . . .

A YOUNG MALE HORSE. (DARLING.) There is also an old age that is both majestic and repulsive.

A YOUNG FEMALE HORSE. The old age which the piebald gelding had reached was of just that sort.

Song: CONVERSATION OF STRIDER
AND THE HERD

STRIDER.
COAL-BLACK STALLION—COULD YOU EVER
UNDERSTAND A PIEBALD STEED?
COAL-BLACK STALLION.
NO—NEVER UNDERSTAND YOU!
STRIDER.
CHESTNUT FILLY—COULD YOU NEVER
KNOW AN ANCIENT WRECK LIKE ME?
CHESTNUT FILLY.
NO—SO I MUST DESPISE YOU!
A MALE HORSE. (*The* GENERAL.) He was old . . .
STRIDER. They were young.
A FEMALE HORSE. He was gaunt.
STRIDER. They were sleek.
VIAZAPURIKHA. He was sad.
STRIDER. They were gay.
A MALE HORSE. And so, he was a strange, alien, utterly different creature; and it was impossible for them to have compassion for him.
STRIDER. Horses pity only themselves, and very occasionally those in whose skins they might easily imagine themselves to be.
A FEMALE HORSE. He was old.
ANOTHER FEMALE HORSE. —And gaunt.
A MALE HORSE (SERPUHOVSKY.) —And ugly.
STRIDER. But am I to blame for that?
A YOUNG MALE HORSE. (DARLING.) One would think not . . . (*General laughter.*) But according to equine ethics he is to blame!
HERD. (ALL.) He is to blame!
THE SAME YOUNG MALE HORSE. —Because only those are blameless who are strong, young and happy.
A FEMALE HORSE. Those who have life still before them!
ANOTHER YOUNG MALE HORSE. (*The* GROOM *rearing up and demonstrating.*) Whose every muscle quivers with over-abundant energy!
A YOUNG FEMALE HORSE. And whose tails stand straight up in the air!

STRIDER. The piebald gelding was the butt of every joke and the laughing stock of the stud farm.

AN OLDER MALE HORSE (SERPUHOVSKY.) He suffered more from the young horses than he did from humans.

A YOUNG FEMALE HORSE. *People* needed him.

STRIDER. He never harmed a living thing. Why then did these young horses torment him so? (*Sings.*)

JUST LIKE WOLVES THESE YOUNGER STALLIONS
AIM TO TEAR SOMEONE APART
HERD. (ALL.)
WE DON'T CARE FOR OLD ONES!
STRIDER.
EVEN NOW THEIR YOUTH IS PASSING
THEY DON'T KNOW THEIR TIME IS SHORT
HERD.
WE DON'T CARE TO HEAR IT!

STRIDER. Yes, I agree I am to blame because I have lived out all my life! I agree I must pay for this life.

A FEMALE HORSE But he was, after all, only a horse.

A MALE HORSE And he could not keep from feeling hurt, and melancholy . . .

STRIDER. . . . and offended by all these young horses who tormented him for the very thing that would befall them at the end of their lives. (*Sings*)

NO, IT ISN'T YOUTH'S ABANDON
THAT MOST TERRIFIES ME NOW—
STRIDER and HERD.
THAT'S THE WAY OF HORSES
STRIDER.
WHAT IS FRIGHT'NING IS THE EVIL
THAT GOES HAND-IN-HAND WITH YOUTH!
STRIDER and HERD.
LIFE IS NEVER EASY!

(STRIDER *sings this at a slower tempo, so that his is the last voice heard, ending the song.*)

STRIDER. It was as if they were learning something new and extraordinary from him.

A FEMALE HORSE. (*Who becomes butterfly prop handler.*) And, indeed, something new and extraordinary was learned from him. (*She exits as the other horses sit.*)

STRIDER. This is what they learned . . . (*A violin plays. The* HERD *gathers around* STRIDER *to listen to and watch the telling of his story.*) When I was born I didn't understand what they meant when they called me a piebald: I thought I was a horse. I remember I kept wanting something. Everything seemed to me very surprising and yet perfectly simple. After nosing around under my mother's belly, I found what I wanted and began to suck. I must have been foaled in the night. Towards dawn, I was already licked clean by my mother, and was standing on my own legs. (*Music.* STRIDER *transforms into a foal on all fours. His tail is retrieved by* VIAZAPURIKHA. *He wobbles and then rolls onto the floor kicking his legs. A member of the* HERD *enters with a paper butterfly on a string attached to a stick. The butterfly is manipulated like a puppet, and* STRIDER *curiously plays with it, finally swallowing it. The butterfly handler exits. The barn door bangs open and casts a shaft of light into the barn. The* GROOM *enters dragging a sack.* STRIDER *comes up behind him and nudges him, as the rest of the* HERD *continue to watch.*)

GROOM. (*Turning around and noticing* STRIDER.) What the . . . why, Baba has foaled! Come look, Vaska! See what she's done—a piebald colt! Just look at all those colors—a perfect magpie! Ekh! The General won't keep him in the stud—he'd ruin the line! Vaska, wake up! (*The* GROOM *and* STRIDER *roll around playing.*) What a shame—a piebald. Why he's completely piebald! We've never had a piebald in the line before! (*He tickles* STRIDER.)

STRIDER. (*Imitating him as if learning to speak.*) P-pie-bald, Ne-i-gh-bald!

GROOM. P-pie-bald.

STRIDER. Neigh-bald.

GROOM. Oh, you want to play do you? (*He flicks his whip slightly at* STRIDER—*the horse's first feeling of pain, the first blow.*)

STRIDER. N-ei-gh-bald.

GROOM That's more like it! See what a lively one he is! There's no holding him! What kind of devil was his sire? He's just like a peasant's horse—a regular muzhik! Stand still a minute! "Muzhik," that's what we'll call him (*Calling to* VASKA *who continues to sleep*) You should feel his hide, Vaska! (*He gets the colt to stand still in a racing pose.*) Muzhik-the-First, by Amiable out of Baba. Such a fine horse—but what a god-damn shame you're so piebald!

STRIDER. "Piebald." (*The barn door bangs open. The GEN-ERAL enters.*)

GROOM. Vaska! Wake up, the General is coming! (*VASKA awakens with great effort and jumps up.*)

VASKA. The best of health to you, your Excellency!

GENERAL. (*Spotting the colt.*) And what is this?

GROOM. Baba foaled last night, your Excellency.

GENERAL. Damn it all, just what I needed—a piebald! What a shame. He's a fine colt, remarkably fine! Damn! There's never been a piebald in the line before! (STRIDER *neighs, everyone laughs.*) Let's see, what will we do with him? . . . Ah, for the time being we'll keep him in the stall with Darling. I'm not keeping him. For now I'll give him to you, Groom! But when he's old enough to breed, I'm warning you, Groom, watch out!

GROOM. Thank you, your Excellency. Thank you very much. He's a fine horse—I'll take good care of him!

GENERAL. But don't forget to take care of *my* horses. They're mine, not yours. That is to say, they are Count Bobrinsky's horses. Remember that. It's very witty. (GENERAL *laughs.* STRIDER *laughs.*)

GROOM. Yes, your Excellency, I will remember that! You'll see—I'll serve you even better than before! I promise, you won't have to worry about anything!

GENERAL. That's better. (*As he exits.*) Yes, he's a fine fellow, but so piebald! I would even say—excessively piebald! (*Exits.* VASKA *then drifts off, following him.*)

GROOM. (*To* STRIDER.) Well, little devil, now you're mine! My horse! Did you hear what the General ordered? To put you in with Darling. But you better watch out! You can play with Darling all you like, lick him with your tongue, but I'm warning you in a nice way—if I see you going after a filly, if I catch you making love . . . (*A whinny from the* HERD, *perhaps from* "Baba.")

STRIDER. L-o-v-e?

GROOM. If I see you've gone after a filly, I'll beat you to death! Is that clear? You're going to be my horse, not the count's. Maybe the General will forget that he only gave you to me for a while. The old count won't miss you—he has a whole stud farm! And I'm going to raise you for myself! Oh, you can

bet I'll take care of you— (*Emotionally.*) you're my horse!
Maybe I'll even keep you for your whole life! The General was
right when he said, "He's a piebald . . . (*He goes back to the
sack and starts to exit.*)

STRIDER. (*Overlapping.*) He kept on saying something to me
for a long time . . .

GROOM . . . but he's still a remarkably fine horse " (*Exits.*)

STRIDER. but I no longer listened. The words I had heard
were enough. There was a great deal about human speech I did
not understand. Particularly the word "love." (VIAZAPURIKHA,
*who has been sitting, listening to the story with the other horses,
now joins* STRIDER *She affectionately offers him back his tail,
which she had retrieved when he had fallen on all fours as a
colt.*)

VIAZAPURIKHA. I was only a filly myself at the time, and I
too . . . oh, what could I, a silly little thing understand then?
Nothing. I understood nothing!

STRIDER. Do you remember, Viazapurikha, do you remember . . .

VIAZAPURIKHA I remember how we learned to nibble grass.

STRIDER. And running around our mothers! Do you
remember?

VIAZAPURIKHA I remember everything. I remember that we
were especially friendly at the beginning.

STRIDER. What?

VIAZAPURIKHA. I said, especially friendly . . .

STRIDER. Don't yell, I can hear you.

VIAZAPURIKHA. but towards the end of autumn . . .

STRIDER. Towards the end of autumn, I remember that you
began to shy away from me.

VIAZAPURIKHA. No, it was you who began to shy away from
me. You would walk clear to the other side.

STRIDER. No, it was you.

VIAZAPURIKHA. Oh, you just don't remember.

STRIDER I remember.

VIAZAPURIKHA. I remember.

STRIDER. (*To the other horses and the audience.*) I will not
try to tell you the whole story of my unhappy first love.
(*Music*) Viazapurikha herself remembers my senseless passion,
which ended in the most important change for me. I fell in love!—
And this caused a terrible thing to happen to me. (*On the*

music cue, VIAZAPURIKHA *has broken away from* STRIDER *and has transformed into young* VIAZAPURIKHA *by letting down her hair and throwing off her shawl.* STRIDER *also becomes a young horse.*)

DUET

VIAZAPURIKHA.
WARM AND TENDER FEELS THE SUN ON MY BACK
STRIDER.
HERE UPON MY SHOULDER, DEAR, LAY YOUR
    HEAD
VIAZAPURIKHA.
NIGHT'S ALMOST OVER—THE WOLVES DO NOT
    HOWL
SO WHY DO YOU LOOK AT ME SHYLY THAT WAY?
STRIDER.
SO WARM AND TENDER FEELS THE SUN ON MY
    BACK
VIAZAPURIKHA.
HERE UPON MY SHOULDER, DEAR, LAY YOUR
    HEAD
STRIDER.
THE WHIP OF THE GROOM HAS BEEN HUNG ON
    THE WALL
SO WHY DO YOU LOOK AT ME SHYLY THAT
    WAY?
VIAZAPURIKHA and STRIDER.
SO WARM AND TENDER FEELS THE SUN ON MY
    BACK
HERE UPON MY SHOULDER, DEAR, LAY YOUR
    HEAD.
VIAZAPURIKHA.
THE GENTLEST TOUCH—
STRIDER.
THE SOFTEST CARESS—
VIAZAPURIKHA.
THE STRANDS OF YOUR MANE—
STRIDER.
ALL ENTANGLED WITH MINE

BOTH.
HOT AS FIRE FEELS THE SUN ON MY BACK
HERE UPON MY SHOULDER, DEAR, LAY YOUR
    HEAD

(*Towards the end of the song, a handsome, young stallion
named* DARLING *has entered. He neighs in approval at their
nuzzling.*)

VIAZAPURIKHA. (*Embarrassed and getting the "giggles."*) Oh,
it's Darling! (*She retreats to a group of fillies and shyly covers
her face with her tail.*)
    DARLING. Go on! Go on! Are you afraid? (*He waves his tail
at the conductor to "cue" the song, he "teaches"* STRIDER *and*
VIAZAPURIKHA *about love.*)

DARLING'S ROMANCE

THERE IS NO ROOM FOR FEAR, MY FRIENDS, IN
    LOVE'S APARTMENTS
SO LISTEN TO ME, LITTLE COLT—DON'T WASTE
    THE SPRINGTIME!
AND IF YOU THINK THIS KIND OF LOVE IS
    PURELY EQUINE—
WHEN PEOPLE SAY 'A STUD' THEY DON'T
    JUST MEAN A HORSE!

SO LITTLE FILLY, LET US LIFT UP OUR TAILS
AND PRANCE UNHINDERED BY A BRIDLE OR
    MANE
AND JUST LET NATURE TAKE ITS NATURAL
    COURSE
FOR LOVE'S A SCIENCE—OR I'M NOT A HORSE!

YOU CALL YOURSELF A HORSE, MY FRIEND
    MEN THINK YOU CUNNING—
YOUR PASSION YET IN EMBERS LIES UNFANN'D
    BY SPRINGTIME
THE GROOM'S OFF SOMEWHERE GETTING
    DRUNK—SO TAKE ADVANTAGE—
WHY DON'T YOU PROVE TO HER YOU REALLY
    ARE A HORSE!

I

SO LITTLE FILLY, LET US LIFT UP OUR TAILS
HOW SWEET TO GAMBOL WITHOUT HARNESS
    OR BIT
AND JUST LET NATURE TAKE ITS NATURAL
    COURSE
FOR LOVE'S A SCIENCE—OR I'M NOT A HORSE!

I'M JUST THE SAME AS YOU, MY FRIEND, WE
    BOTH ARE STALLIONS
WE WHINNY AS WE ANSWER BACK THE CALL OF
    SPRINGTIME—
TILL RIPPLES DAPPLE ALL OUR SKIN, OUR
    NOSTRILS FLAMING—
WHEN PASSION COMES TO LIFE, THERE'S NOTHING
    LIKE A HORSE!

SO LITTLE FILLY LET US LIFT UP OUR TAILS
ENJOY THE FREEDOM TO MAKE LOVE LIKE A
    BEAST
AND JUST LET NATURE TAKE ITS NATURAL
    COURSE—
IF LOVE'S NO SCIENCE THEN I'M NOT A HORSE!

(*At the end of the song,* DARLING *breaks away.* STRIDER *and*
VIAZAPURIKHA *are once again old.* DARLING *prances and
assumes various poses as* STRIDER *describes him.*)

STRIDER. (*Telling his story to the other horses and to the
audience.*) Darling was a fine saddle horse. Later he was ridden
by the Tsar himself and portrayed in paintings and statues. But
then . . .

VIAZAPURIKHA. (*Yearningly*) . . . but then he was just a
yearling with a silky coat, a swanlike neck, and legs—straight
and slender, taut as violin strings.

STRIDER. (*Testily.*) You remember him very well!

VIAZAPURIKHA. He was carefree and handsome.

STRIDER He was frivolous

VIAZAPURIKHA. He was always ready to frolic, lick with his
tongue, or play tricks on horses or men.

DARLING. (*To them, and to the audience.*) We know how to
love. We are animals!

STRIDER. We were friends. We became friends living in the same stall, and we would have remained friends through our entire youth if he and Viazapurikha . . .

VIAZAPURIKHA. No, don't tell!

STRIDER. Ah! You do remember! (*Quietly.*) We had a race . . .

VIAZAPURIKHA. The race . . . (*The lights change again, and they become young horses again. They stand around bored, switching their tails at flies, etc.*)

DARLING. (*Suddenly*) Let's have a race! (*Music.*)

STRIDER. I'll race you!

VIAZAPURIKHA. (*Leaping ahead, the others pull her back.*) I l-o-v-e to race!

DARLING. I'll win!

STRIDER. Don't be too sure.

DARLING. You'll see. I'm a racer!

STRIDER. Ready, set—go! (*The race begins The horses sitting and listening to the story follow it with enthusiasm.* STRIDER *runs off in the lead* DARLING *and* VIAZAPURIKHA *follow him.* STRIDER *exits.* DARLING *and* VIAZAPURIKHA *run off, following* STRIDER. STRIDER *appears again and races off. The other two appear, beginning to tire. They slow down to catch their breaths, and laugh and nuzzle each other as they circle, playfully at first and then with gradual sexual awareness.* VIAZAPURIKHA *leaps off to continue the race.* DARLING *becomes aware of his feelings, then stretches out and holds up his tail, racing off to catch up with* VIAZAPURIKHA. STRIDER *runs on breathlessly and looks behind him, thinking that he's ahead of the others and that he's won. He runs off to finish the race. The couple run on together, giggling and laughing in a subdued, after-making-love way They lie on the ground together, resting on one another, contentedly relaxed.* STRIDER *runs on the way he ran off, victorious* VIAZAPURIKHA *and* DARLING *soon become aware of his presence as he watches them*)

DARLING. (*Seeing* STRIDER) Boy, you're fast! (STRIDER *is upset.* VIAZAPURIKHA *goes over to him trying playfully to nuzzle him*)

STRIDER. (*Tensely.*) Why did you do that?

VIAZAPURIKHA. What?

STRIDER. Why did you do that with him?

DARLING. (*Simply.*) We are animals!

VIAZAPURIKHA. (*Like a petulant adolescent making an excuse.*) I was tired. I couldn't keep up with you.

STRIDER. Why did you do that with him? Why not with me? What's wrong with me?

VIAZAPURIKHA. They call you a pie . . . a pie . . . (*To* DARLING.) What's the word?

DARLING. A pie . . . bald.

VIAZAPURIKHA. That's right. I'm afraid of you!

STRIDER. (*Deeply neighing in anguish.*) No-o-o . . . No-o-o . . . No-o-o! (VIAZAPURIKHA *and* DARLING *run away from him. He looks at* VIAZAPURIKHA) Come here! . . . Come here! (VIAZAPURIKHA *goes over to him slowly.*) We are animals! (STRIDER *grabs* VIAZAPURIKHA. *She struggles and is thrown to the ground with* STRIDER *above her. The* HERD *circles around them, masking* STRIDER *and* VIAZAPURIKHA. VIAZAPURIKHA *whinnies, then it is silent. The* HERD *flick their tails.*)

GENERAL. (*Off.*) Groom! Groom! (*A cowbell is heard.*)

GROOM. (*Enters, rushes over, pulls* STRIDER *away from* VIAZAPURIKHA *and disperses the other horses to their stalls.*) Why you . . . I'll get you for this! Get away from there! I'll kill you!

VASKA. (*Clanging a cow bell.*) The General! The General! The General is coming! (*The* GENERAL *enters.* VIAZAPURIKHA *limps back to her stall and is nuzzled by another horse.* STRIDER *goes toward her to see if she is alright, but* VIAZAPURIKHA *rears up at him.*)

GENERAL. (*Enraged.*) Groom, did you let the colt loose?

GROOM. Not at all, your Excellency . . .

GENERAL. Silence! (*He goes over to* STRIDER, *examines him and realizes what has happened.*) I'll have everyone flogged for this!

GROOM. (*Frightened.*) I didn't order him to be let loose. One of the stable boys must have let him out!

GENERAL No alibis . . . (*Raising his whip.*) Stable boy? Which stable boy?

GROOM. Vaska. (VASKA *tries to leave. The cowbell clanging in* VASKA's *hand gives him away*)

GENERAL. Vaska, come here! (VASKA *comes nearer.*) Were you drunk?

VASKA. Was I drunk? . . . No, I wasn't drunk, your Excellency . . .

GENERAL. Silence! Are you trying to excuse yourself?

GROOM. (*Apologetically for* VASKA.) He didn't feed the horses last night, your Excellency. He was celebrating It was a holiday   . . St. George's Day.

GENERAL. A holiday A holiday. We'll give him a holiday he'll never forget! Give it to him! Give it to him and I'm going to watch! (*He shoves the* GROOM *towards* VASKA.)

VASKA. Your Excellency . . . Your Excellency . . . Why? Because of this piebald colt? He's not yours, and he's not the Count's either As if I would neglect your horses or the Count's! But this, your Excellency   . . this colt belongs to him—the stud groom! It's his! I confess I was drunk, but I would never forget to feed a colt that was yours, even in that condition . . . And this one I simply forgot. But he's not yours, and he's not the Count's. That's why he got so restless—from hunger! But now I ll never let him out with the others for anything. I'll be careful. (*He falls on his knees.*) But Excellency . . . the colt isn't even yours . . . and he's not the Count's!

GENERAL. Silence! There must be equality and justice—and someone must be punished! And you're still drunk!

VASKA. Excellency! . . .

GENERAL. No alibis! Silence! (DARLING *whinnies. The* GENERAL *walks toward his stall and gives him a piece of sugar.*) Beautiful! What a beauty. (DARLING *bites his hand and retreats to his stall. The* GENERAL *shouts in pain and returns to the* GROOM) Give it to him, and give it to him good! As for that piebald   . . (*The* GENERAL *gestures for the* GROOM *to follow him and leaves. The* GROOM *follows the* GENERAL *off, then after a beat, returns.*)

GROOM Vaska! Come on, get going.

VASKA. But the colt isn't even the Count's . . . (*The* GROOM *drags* VASKA *off to be flogged. The sound of the whipping is heard The* HERD, *reacting to each blow, neighs, rears up on their hind legs, etc. The audience sees them in silhouette on each leg of the stalls.*)

GROOM'S VOICE. I'll show you "not the Count's!"

VASKA'S VOICE. You have no Christian soul! (*Whip.*) A beast has more pity from you than a man! (*Whip.*) You're an infidel! (*More whips. The* GROOM *and the flogged* VASKA *re-enter—the* GROOM *half-carries* VASKA, *supporting him over his own back.*)

VASKA. Barbarian! The General himself never flogged me so hard. My whole back's been plowed up! You have no Christian soul!

GROOM. Silence! Are you still making excuses? (*He leaves the barn again.*)

VASKA. Aaah! You piebald beast! If it wasn't for you, nothing would have happened! (*Goes to* STRIDER *and suddenly kicks him full force in the stomach. The* GROOM *returns with ropes and leads* STRIDER *to the Center of the stage.*)

GROOM. (*Simply.*) Vaska, come here.

VASKA. What now?

GROOM. (*Simply.*) We're going to geld him.

VASKA. What?

GROOM. The General's ordered it. (STRIDER *is blindfolded with a black cloth. Each arm and leg is roped and various members of the* HERD *hold the ends of the ropes, pulling them taut to the edges of the stage. A rope is placed around his middle which also extends to the sides of the stage. The* GROOM *and* VASKA *put on leather aprons, preparing for the operation. The* HERD *sings as* STRIDER *is roped and blindfolded.*)

HERD.

OH, CRUEL AND HARD OF HEART IS MAN
HE'S BORN AND DIES IN BLOOD
HE KILLED THE SPIRIT OF THE HORSE
AND LEFT HIS FLESH ALIVE

JUST YESTERDAY HIS NEIGH RANG OUT
AND LIFE WAS FULL OF JOY
BUT NOW HIS SOUL IS IN DESPAIR
HIS SEED FOREVER LOST

(*The* GROOM *and* VASKA, *with knife in hand, slowly approach* STRIDER. *There is a shriek and a blackout. The horses have all reacted with neighs, food-stamping and whinnies. Out of the darkness and the horse sounds, a high tenor voice is heard singing a musical lament. When it has died away, the lights come up and* STRIDER *is standing alone unroped.* STRIDER *removes his blindfold in silence, then talks to the* HERD *and the audience.*)

STRIDER. The following day, I stopped neighing forever. I became what I am now. The whole world was changed to my eyes. Nothing was sweet to me. I withdrew into myself and began to think. Sometimes I would get the urge to kick up my heels, to roll over, to whinny, but then came the dreadful question: "Why? What for?" and all the life would go out of me. One evening, just as the herd was being driven back from the fields, I was taken out for a walk. I saw all our brood mares, and heard them laughing and stamping their hoofs I stopped short, and gazed at the approaching herd as one gazes at a happiness that is lost forever and will never return again. I forgot myself, and neighed in the old way out of habit. But my neighing sounded sad, comical, unbecoming. None of my old friends laughed, but many of them, out of politeness turned away. Suddenly I understood everything: How I had become a stranger to them forever. (*Pause. He is silently weeping.*) I don't remember how I came home . . . (*A* FEMALE HERD MEMBER/ GYPSY WOMAN *has entered. She sings, accompanying herself on the guitar.*)

GYPSY WOMAN. (HERD MEMBER)
OH HARD IS LIFE FOR MAN AND HORSE
BUT AS THE YEARS GALLOP BY
YOU'LL VALUE SIMPLE PLEASURES BEST
LIKE GRASS—AND DRINK—AND WARMTH

STRIDER. I reflected on the injustice of the humans, who blamed me for being piebald. I reflected on the inconstancy of female love. And most of all, I reflected on that strange breed of animal with whom we are so closely bound, and whom we call "men." (*He has tied his blindfold into a bowtie.*) I could not understand at all what it meant when they spoke of *me* as the property of a man . . . as if there were some sort of bond between me and the stud groom. To say "my horse" in reference to me, a living horse, seemed as strange to me as to say, "my earth," "my air," "my water . . ." (*The barn door bangs open.*)

GROOM'S VOICE. Vaska!

VASKA'S VOICE. Huh?

GROOM. (*Appearing.*) Come on, let's harness him. (*The* GROOM *has a harness and a bit.* STRIDER *fights for his last vestige of freedom. Once harnessed, he is still.*)

VASKA. (*During the harnessing.*) Well, now, what are you up to you devil? He's going to kick now! Whoa! Whoa! Alright, fella!

GROOM. Watch those hind legs—he'll kick alright!

VASKA. No he won't. He's broken now.

GROOM. Yes, now he's broken. My, but you were a spirited devil. Now you're quiet. (*Taking* STRIDER's *head.*) Hey, Vaska, why the hell did you tear him? Look at that lip?

VASKA. I tore his lip? He ripped it himself against the bit!

GROOM. (*Mimicking him.*) "Ripped it himself against the bit." Come on, finish harnessing him. I'm driving to Chesmenka. (*To* STRIDER.) You're my horse.

VASKA. What are you doing in Chesmenka?

GROOM. I have business there. (*He leaves.*)

VASKA. (*Calling after the* GROOM.) I know your business in Chesmenka. You have a woman there—your "filly." (*He laughs and exits after the* GROOM.)

STRIDER. (*Holding up reins in a wide gesture.*) "My horse (*He tugs on each strap.*) . . . my . . . mine." These words had a profound effect on my life. Their meaning is this: human beings enjoy talking about things using the words "my" and "mine " And, they have agreed that only one human may use this word "mine" about any particular thing. He who can say "mine" about the greatest number of things is considered the happiest. Why this is so, I do not know, but it is so. After broadening my horizons, I became convinced that, in respect not only to horses, but to all things, this notion of "my" and "mine" is nothing more than a low, primitive human instinct which they call the sense or right of private property. There are men who say "my house," yet they've never lived in it; "my land," yet they've never walked on it; "my people" yet they do their people harm. (*Shaking his head.*) On the scale of animal intelligence, horses stand at least a rung higher than men. I was three times unfortunate: I was a piebald, I was a gelding, and men imagined that I did not belong to God and myself, as is natural to every living thing, but that I belonged to the stud groom. "My . . . mine." I made many observations of men during the time I was passed from hand to hand. I was held the longest by Prince Serpuhovsky . . . (*Music.* SERPUHOVSKY *has entered smoking a cigar*) an officer of the Hussars. This is how it began (STRIDER *exits.* VASKA *and the* GROOM *bring on an imposing chair and place it in the center of the barn for the* PRINCE *The* GENERAL *follows them on. An inspection of horses for a sale begins as the* PRINCE *sits.*)

GENERAL. Groom! (*He cracks his whip. The* GROOM *leads out one of the horses.*) This is the one, Prince, that I bought from Voikoff.

SERPUHOVSKY. From Voikoff? Terrible. (*He notices* STRIDER, *who does not participate in the showing, but who has entered to do his work of hauling sacks and piling them up near his post.* STRIDER *is casually dragging one sack across the floor when* SERPUHOVSKY's *and* STRIDER's *glances meet. During the scene,* STRIDER *passes behind the* PRINCE *as he crosses back and forth doing his work,* VASKA *helps the* GROOM *return the horses to their stalls, getting the next one ready to show, etc The* GROOM *leads out another horse.*) Whose little white-legged filly is that? Pretty animal. (STRIDER *crosses behind the* PRINCE *again, exiting to get more sacks*)

GENERAL. That's still a strain of my old Khrenovsky racers.

SERPUHOVSKY. She's spirited, pleasing, but—no offense—I must say that she is not the best example of that breed.

GENERAL. You don't think so?

SERPUHOVSKY. Believe me! (STRIDER *enters carrying another sack and piles it up by the post.*)

GENERAL. (*Cracking his whip.*) Groom, show the chestnut mare and the coal-black stallion. (*The* GROOM *leads out two horses from a stall. They march around as a team and display various balancing steps.*)

SERPUHOVSKY. (*Glancing at them briefly.*) They're yearlings, aren't they? No, I don't like them either. (STRIDER *exits to get more sacks.*)

GENERAL. I have another thought. (*To* GROOM.) Hey there! Bring out the roan stallion. (STRIDER, *noticing the* PRINCE's *attention, has entered carrying two sacks; one under each arm.*)

GROOM The roan?

GENERAL. The roan, the roan! (*He shoves the* GROOM *towards the horse. The* GROOM *brings out a spirited and resistant roan, but* SERPUHOVSKY *continues to gaze at* STRIDER.) Here, Prince—I think this one should suit you perfectly. (*The* PRINCE *looks at the* GENERAL *with obvious dissatisfaction.* STRIDER *has exited to get more sacks.*) You're right. I confess I'm guilty! Alright then, Groom, bring out you-know-who! (*The* GROOM *goes off through a stall. The* GENERAL *cracks his whip. We hear a musical chord, and* DARLING *leaps out Music* DARLING *dances around the* PRINCE *as the* GROOM *tries to keep up with him on the other end of the rope.* DARLING *stops near the* PRINCE's *chair in a final pose.* STRIDER *has also stopped by the chair, carrying three sacks on his head.*) And now, what do you think of our Darling?

SERPUHOVSKY. Truly handsome. He's got spark. But his gait —not so good. Too precious. (DARLING, *indignant at his rejection, motions to the* GROOM *with a haughty gesture of his tail to be led off.* STRIDER *continues to stack up the sacks.*)

GENERAL. Well then, I really don't know how to please you.

SERPUHOVSKY. Let me see that one closer. (*Indicates* STRIDER.)

GENERAL. Which one?

SERPUHOVSKY. That one, closer. (STRIDER *looks around the post in the direction the* PRINCE *has been pointing, then realizes it is himself.*)

GENERAL. You can't be serious, Prince. Why, here's Darling! (*The* GENERAL *cracks his whip,* DARLING *again leaps out on a musical chord.*)

SERPUHOVSKY. I said bring him closer! (DARLING *is yanked off mid-leap.*)

GENERAL. Groom, closer! (*He motions to the* GROOM *to do so.* STRIDER *is led to center where the* PRINCE *begins to examine him.*)

SERPUHOVSKY. What a patchwork he is. (*To* STRIDER.) Come on, show me your hoof! (*After a slight pause,* STRIDER *coyly decides to show it to him.*) Why aren't his hooves oiled?

GENERAL. Groom, why aren't his hooves oiled?

GROOM. I'm sorry, your Excellency!

GENERAL. You *will* be sorry. (*The* GROOM *bends down to be flogged, baring his back.*) Later!

SERPUHOVSKY. General, my mind's made up. I'm taking this patchwork, here.

GENERAL. The piebald?

SERPUHOVSKY. The piebald.

GENERAL. The piebald.

SERPUHOVSKY. The piebald.

GENERAL. You must be joking, Prince!

SERPUHOVSKY. No, General, I'm not joking. I like him. No one has such a colorful horse. When we ride through the streets, all Moscow will stare at us! (*The* PRINCE *leads* STRIDER *around the barn. The other horses show amusement or disdain.* STRIDER *struts on the* PRINCE'S *arm, clearly enjoying the attention.*)

GENERAL Prince, I honestly wanted to please you, but now I understand: it is not refinement you seek, but originality. Believe me, a horse is not a commodity one acquires to be fashionable There *are* no fashions in horses!

SERPUHOVSKY. But I want to be fashionable!

GENERAL. Now I see that you are a true Hussar, Prince. It is very wittty. (*He laughs, clapping the* PRINCE *on the shoulder with too much familiarity.*)

SERPUHOVSKY. (*Freezing the* GENERAL'S *laugh and his touch with a glance*) It is not wittty, at all. General, you yourself said, "Choose any one you like from the herd." So, I chose one. What more is there to say?

GENERAL True indeed! But you never even looked at Darling. This is Darling! (*The* GENERAL *cracks his whip.* DARLING *leaps out on a musical chord, this time with* VASKA *in tow. Once again, he dances around the chair and over to the* PRINCE, *giving him a kiss on the cheek as the music ends*)

SERPUHOVSKY. Charmant! But I choose this one. (*Darling kicks him and exits in a huff.*) Now tell me, what do I owe you?

GENERAL. For this one . . . the piebald?

SERPUHOVSKY Yes. The patchwork one.

GENERAL. The patchwork . . . Yes . . . it would have been more appropriate if I had lost him to you in a card game, dear friend. Groom! . . . How much?

GROOM. (*Hesitates.*) Eight hundred?

GENERAL. Eight hundred rubles, Prince. That's the price.

SERPUHOVSKY. That isn't money, that's a fleabite.

GENERAL Groom, a while ago I gave you this horse as a gift, so I guess it's your windfall—take it! Now am I not an honorable man?

GROOM I'm most obliged to you, your Excellency. (*He bows.*) I'll never forget this. (*The* GROOM *runs off after the* GENERAL, *leaping after the money which the* GENERAL *teasingly holds beyond his reach.* VASKA *follows them. Alone together,* SERPUHOVSKY *and* STRIDER *gaze into each others' eyes.*)

SERPUHOVSKY So, my patchwork gelding—you are mine. Do you like that? Does that please you? (STRIDER *makes a horse sound, blowing air through his lips and vibrating them The* PRINCE *imitates the sound. They communicate, making the*

sound, back and forth to each other. They both begin to laugh.
Feofan!

FEOFAN. (*Appears from nowhere.*) Right!

SERPUHOVSKY. Let's go home. (*Music. As* FEOFAN *hitches the reins to* STRIDER'S *harness, the* HERD *clears the stage of the chair and sacks. Some* HERD *members sit and watch this part of the story.* FEOFAN *and* STRIDER *parade around the stage as* STRIDER *performs a seductive dance entrancing the* PRINCE. *They stop to pick up the* PRINCE *in an imaginary carriage created by the reins.*) Allez!

FEOFAN. Let her go! (*THE RIDE HOME:* STRIDER *trots slowly at first, eventually showing off his trot, his cantor and his gallop with dance-like steps.*)

SERPUHOVSKY Let him run a little—see what he can do. (*The tempo accelerates and so do they.*) Let him out, Feofan! Give him his head! (*The tempo is at its fastest.* STRIDER *leaps over two "bumps" in the road.* FEOFAN *and the* PRINCE *jump over the same "bumps" in the carriage.* FEOFAN *brings the carriage to a halt.*)

FEOFAN. Whoa! Boy, you're a racer. Good for you, Spots! (*He unhitches* STRIDER.)

SERPUHOVSKY. Yes, he certainly is colorful! (*They exit in different directions.*)

STRIDER. (*To the audience.*) I spent the happiest years of my life with the Hussar. Though he was the cause of my destruction, though he never loved anything or anyone, yet I loved him, and still love him, for that very reason. What pleased me most was that he was handsome, happy and rich, and therefore never loved anybody. (*Personally to the audience.*) You can understand that: it is the most fulfilling emotion that we horses have. His coldness, his cruelty and my complete dependence on him gave a special strength to my love for him. "Kill me," I used to think in those days; (*Music.*) "Drive me to death! I shall be all the happier." (FEOFAN *and the* PRINCE *return from either side of the stage. Each carries an identical table—*FEOFAN'S *has grooming equipment, the* PRINCE'S *has toilette articles upon it.*)

SERPUHOVSKY'S SONG

SERPUHOVSKY. (*Preparing to shave. Sings.*)
IF YOU HOPE FOR EV'RYONE TO FEAR YOU
FEAR YOU NO ONE ON YOUR PART

IF YOU LONG FOR EV'RYONE TO LOVE YOU
NEVER EVER GIVE YOUR HEART!
NIGHT IS YOUNG AND FAST OUR STEED, MY
    FRIEND
NO OTHER BIBLE DO WE NEED, MY FRIEND
(*The music continues to accompany the scene.*) Feofan!
Blacken his hooves, put the brightest blanket on him, curry him
thoroughly, and we're off to the races! (*He begins to shave.*)

FEOFAN. Well, you beast, don't forget! Look cheerful, now—
handsome is as handsome does!

STRIDER. Those were the best days of my life. He had a
mistress. I know, because I took him to her every day, and I
took her out driving. She was a bareback rider in the circus. Her
name was Mme. Mathieu.

SERPUHOVSKY. (*Looking at a photograph.*) Ah, Mathieu!
(*Kisses it, then wipes the shaving cream off the picture.*)

STRIDER She was a handsome woman, and he was handsome,
and his coachman was handsome, and I loved them all because
they were And life was worth living then This is the way I
would spend my day. In the morning, Feofan, the head coachman, would come to me. He was a young fellow, taken from the
peasants. (*The* PRINCE *takes a goblet of wine from his toilette
table and gargles.*)

FEOFAN. Here, drink some water, you beast. You must be
thirsty! (*He holds a bowl for* STRIDER *to drink from.* STRIDER,
hearing the PRINCE *gargling, also gargles. They catch each
others' eyes in mutual enjoyment*)

SERPUHOVSKY. Feofan! (*He throws* FEOFAN *a towel to wipe*
STRIDER's *mouth. While the* PRINCE *is trimming his moustache
and looking into his hand mirror,* FEOFAN *notices that something
is bothering* STRIDER *who has made a whimpering sound. The*
PRINCE *comes over to him, sees that it is an annoying whisker
and, using the mirror and his moustache scissors, trims it for
the horse.* STRIDER *nuzzles the* PRINCE *in loving appreciation.*)

STRIDER. Feofan would open the stable door, let out the
steam from the horses, shovel out the manure, take off my
blanket, and brush my back with a currycomb, over and over
again. (FEOFAN *begins to brush* STRIDER *as the* PRINCE *brushes
his own hair.*)

SERPUHOVSKY. Tell me, Feofan, my friend, do you like this
patchwork horse or not?

FEOFAN. I like him. I like him very much.

SERPUHOVSKY. So do I. And the General—he's a fool. He manages a stud farm, but he doesn't know a horse from an ox. I smelled that out right away!

FEOFAN. He's a great horse for eight hundred rubles. That's practically nothing!

SERPUHOVSKY. That's what I say. Eight hundred rubles for such an animal. That's not money, that's a flea bite. (*Sings.*)
EACH LIVING THING FROM DIETY TO
    EARTHWORM
SHOWS UP IN THE MARKETPLACE
BUY IT—SELL IT—WHAT ELSE IS IT GOOD FOR?
ONLY KEEP A HORSE TO RACE!
WHEN THE TROIKA'S RUNNING FREE, MY FRIEND
THAT'S THE TRINITY FOR ME, MY FRIEND!
Just look at this beauty! (STRIDER *assumes various poses.*) Take a look at his legs! The bone is as slender and as straight as an arrow, I noticed that at once! And the neck . . . and the rump . . . and the back!

FEOFAN. It's so broad, you can sleep on it!

SERPUHOVSKY. Yes you can! You really can sleep on it!

STRIDER. Neither one nor the other feared anyone or loved anyone except themselves; therefore everybody loved them.

SERPUHOVSKY and FEOFAN. (*Sing.*)
IF YOU HOPE FOR EV'RYONE TO FEAR YOU
FEAR YOU NO ONE ON YOUR PART
IF YOU LONG FOR EV'RYONE TO LOVE YOU
NEVER EVER GIVE YOUR HEART!
NIGHT IS YOUNG AND FAST OUR STEED, MY
    FRIEND

SERPUHOVSKY.
NO OTHER BIBLE DO WE . . .

FEOFAN.
NO OTHER BIBLE DO WE . . .

STRIDER. (*Makes a horse whinny sound like "NO OTHER BIBLE DO WE . . ."*)

ALL THREE.
NEED MY FRIEND!
(*At the end of the song, a musical watch chime is heard. It plays a melody, then starts to strike the hour. This sound is*

performed by a member of the orchestra. The PRINCE *looks at an elaborate pocket watch.*)

SERPUHOVSKY. Twelve o'clock, Feofan. Hurry up, we'll be late for the races. (FEOFAN *goes off and brings on a troika harness made from blue ribbons, and puts it on* STRIDER.)

STRIDER. It was winter, and I was hitched to a sleigh. But what a sleigh! It was made of plaited cane, upholstered with velvet; the harness had little silver buckles and the reins—pure silk.

SERPUHOVSKY. The forelock, the forelock, don't forget to wet his forelock!

FEOFAN. Rest assured, I won't forget. The best harness today or the second best?

SERPUHOVSKY. The best! After the races, we'll dash over to Stozhenka Street and pay a call on Madame Mathieu.

FEOFAN. Ah Mathieu!

STRIDER. (*Making a horse-like sound that sounds like the words.*) Ah Mathieu!

FEOFAN. (*With an obscene gesture.*) To Mattie then! To Mattie it shall be! I don't care if we go to the Devil, or God himself in Paradise! (*He has exited with his grooming table.*)

STRIDER. Feofan would come out, his backside wider than his shoulders . . .

FEOFAN. (*Returns wearing his coachman's cape and carrying a whip.*) Oh ho ho, you bag of fleas! Wait till we get going, I'll make you see stars, you Devil! Here, take a look at this! (FEOFAN *cracks his whip on the floor and "freezes."*)

STRIDER. Sometimes, he would crack his whip at me—never so as to hurt, only as a joke. I could always take a joke, so I would lay back my ears and gnash my teeth. (*He does so.*)

SERPUHOVSKY. (*From Offstage.*) Hurry up, Feofan! Hurry with the harnessing! Hitch them up! (*Two other horses come out and step into the reins behind* STRIDER. FEOFAN *takes the reins.*)

STRIDER. Feofan would hitch the two coal-black stallions to the troika behind me. And then . . .

FEOFAN. Let her go! (*The troika circles around the stage— as if going from the barn to the main house. The sound of sleigh bells rhythmically marks the horses's steps. Other actors join the scene.*)

STRIDER. (*As they turn Upstage.*) Frisking with each step, I would prance out of the gate. And the cook, who had come out to empty the slops, would stop dead in the doorway!

FEOFAN. (*To the invisible* COOK.) Hey Masha, don't stand there with your mouth wide open! My dearest Mashenka, my blue-eyed sweetie!

STRIDER. And the peasants, bringing firewood into the courtyard, would stare in amazement!

FEOFAN. Watch out! Get out of the way! (*Some of the actors playing the "peasants" cross the stage.*)

STRIDER. In those days there was none of that silly habit of shouting "forward!" As if we didn't know that we went "forward" instead of "backwards!"

FEOFAN. (*Stopping the "sleigh" Downstage, getting out and talking to the audience.*) Feofan, would cluck his tongue, drive up to the door, get off the driver's seat, and casually, carelessly, as if there was nothing exceptional about the sleigh, or the horse . . .

STRIDER. . . . or Feofan himself! And . . .

FEOFAN. And . . .

SERPUHOVSKY. (*Entering in a beautiful cape and hat.*) . . . and the Prince would come out, with a shako on his head, and a velvet cloak with a high collar hiding his rosy, young handsome face . . .

STRIDER. (*Lovingly.*) Which never should have been hidden at all!

FEOFAN. (*To the audience*) Let's not overdo it . . .

SERPUHOVSKY. The Prince would come out, clattering his sabre, his spurs and the brass backs of his boots, striding over the carpet as if in a hurry and taking no notice of Feofan or Patchwork—whom everybody but he looked at and admired. (*He climbs into the troika.*)

FEOFAN. Feofan clucked his tongue.

STRIDER. I would tug at the reins. And with a dignified trot—but not too dignified—away we would go.

FEOFAN. (*Setting the pace.*) Hey . . . hup! . . . hup! . . . hup! . . .

STRIDER. Hup! . . . hup! . . . hup! . . . with wider and wider strides, every muscle quivering, kicking muddy snow on to the dashboard, off I would go! (*Music. The "troika" slowly begins to move out with the* PRINCE *seated in it. During this sequence, what starts as a simple ride becomes a faster and more ferocious race through the streets of Moscow. The troika at first takes pedestrians by surprise. They leap to safety. Later, others are trampled under the horses' hooves and crawl off. Toward the end of the race, other horses and riders and sleighs try to catch up with the troika, but are left behind as* STRIDER *pulls ahead and wins.*)

STRIDER. (*Sings.*)
ALONG THE BLACKSMITH'S ALLEY—LORD, HOW
    WE WOULD FLY!
FEOFAN. (*Joins in.*)
WOE TO SLOWER HORSES—
SERPUHOVSKY. (*Joins in.*)
WOE TO PASSERS-BY
ALL THREE.
DON'T GET IN THE WAY OF OUR AMUSEMENTS
    OR YOU'LL DIE
LOOK OUT—JUMP CLEAR—
AND WE'LL LET YOU LIVE ANOTHER DAY!
    FEOFAN. Watch out! Get out of the way!
    THE ENTIRE COMPANY. (*Singing.*)
CROSS THE BRIDGE AND GIVE THE CROWD A
    SCARE
WE'VE NO TIME FOR BOREDOM OR DESPAIR!
THEN WE HEARD THE DEVIL YELLING SOMETHING
    FROM THE CLOUDS—
LOOK OUT—JUMP CLEAR—
RACE ON THROUGH AND DEVIL TAKE THE CROWD!
    FEOFAN. Watch out! Get out of the way!
    STRIDER & COMPANY. (*Singing.*)
NOW OUR SPEED'S UP—CARE HAS BLOWN AWAY
LET THE WHOLE WORLD DISAPPEAR TODAY!
IT WOULDN'T DO YOU ANY GOOD TO PULL IN
    ON THE REINS—
LOOK OUT—JUMP CLEAR
NOW THE REINS DO AS THE HORSES SAY!
    FEOFAN. Watch out! Get out of the way!
    STRIDER & COMPANY. (*Singing.*)
ALONG THE BLACKSMITH'S ALLEY—LORD, HOW
    WE WOULD FLY!
WOE TO SLOWER HORSES—WOE TO PASSERS-BY

DON'T GET IN THE WAY OF OUR AMUSEMENTS
  OR YOU'LL DIE
LOOK OUT—JUMP CLEAR—
HEY!
(*Music and singing ends abruptly as* STRIDER *has pulled ahead.
  All freeze.*)

STRIDER. (*In a deprecating fashion.*) I lived that way for
only two years.

BLACKOUT

END OF ACT ONE

ACT TWO

(*As the orchestra completes the entre-act, four members of the* CHORUS/HERD *come out.* STRIDER *enters and goes to his post. He wears his harness.* VASKA *enters and lies down as he did in Act One. We hear the sound of light rain.*)

VASKA. (*Sings.*)
OH JESUS—IT'S TIME TO TAKE OUT THE NAGS!
BECAUSE OF THIS DUMB ANIMAL IT SEEMS
I NEVER GET TO FINISH HALF MY DREAMS
OH JESUS—IT'S TIME TO TAKE OUT THE NAGS!

FIRST CHORUS WOMAN. The weather began to change.

FIRST CHORUS MAN. The sky was overcast, and in the morning there was no dew.

SECOND CHORUS WOMAN. It was humid, and the mosquitos were troublesome.

SECOND CHORUS MAN. Then a drizzle began to fall.

FIRST CHORUS WOMAN. In the evening, when the gates were closed, and everything grew quiet, the piebald gelding continued his story. (*The* CHORUS/HERD *members sit to listen.*)

STRIDER. My happy life ended all too soon. I lived this way for only two years. At the end of the second winter, I experienced the most joyous event of my life, and it was quickly followed by my deepest sorrow. "To Stozhenka Street," cried the Prince And away we flew! (*Music. A member of the* HERD *rushes on and rolls out an oriental rug. Another member carries on pillows and places them on the rug, creating the boudoir of Mme. Mathieu.*) This was his mistress's apartment . . . (STRIDER *enjoys the scene, perhaps joining in from the sidelines. On a musical phrase,* SERPUHOVSKY *enters with* MATHIEU. *She is played by the same actress as* VIAZAPURIKHA *and wears a tu-tu and tights—her circus costume.* FEOFAN *and three* GYPSIES *enter; the latter playing mandolins and guitars,* FEOFAN *enters carrying silver champagne glasses on a tray. The* GYPSIES *play a musical introduction. During the song, the* PRINCE, *who is drunk, alternates between enthusiasm for* MATHIEU *and his drink.* MATHIEU, *who wants to make love, becomes increasingly frustrated.*)

37

SERPUHOVSKY'S ROMANCE

SERPUHOVSKY. (*Singing in the gypsy fashion.*)
NEVER GRIEVE FOR WHAT IS PAST—HERE IS WHY,
     MY SWEET
FOR THE CANDLE'S BURNING ON AS WE CRY, MY
     SWEET
BARE YOUR SHOULDER AND MY SORROW WILL
     FLY, MY SWEET
GYPSIES.
BARE YOUR SHOULDER AND MY SORROW WILL
     FLY, MY SWEET
MATHIEU. Charmante! (*She reclines on the pillows.* SER-
PUHOVSKY *kneels above her. Throughout the song, the* GYPSIES
and MATHIEU *try to put the* PRINCE *in a romantic frame of
mind.*)
SERPUHOVSKY (*Sings.*)
POUR THE WINE AND DRAIN THE CUP—LIVE
     TONIGHT, MY SWEET
FOR MORALITY MUST SPRING FROM DELIGHT,
     MY SWEET
AND WHATEVER FEELS ALL RIGHT MUST BE
     RIGHT, MY SWEET!
GYPSIES.
AND, WHATEVER FEELS ALL RIGHT MUST BE
     RIGHT, MY SWEET!
SERPUHOVSKY.
I DRANK BUT NEVER TASTED SUCH SWEET
     INTOXICATION
WE HAVE NO NEED FOR SOULS
OUR FLESH IS OUR CONSCIENCE, MY SWEET

LIVING WITHOUT MATTHEW, WITHOUT LUKE
LIFE GOES BY SO QUICKLY
WHEN THEY CLOSE YOUR EYES WITH SILVER
     COINS
IT'S TOO LATE TO START TO LIVE!
MATHIEU. Ah, Prince, why do you sing of death? Either love
or death. Ah, mon Prince, pourquoi tu parles de la morte? La
morte ou l'amour! Non, non c'est affreux!
FEOFAN. (*Comes to* MATHIEU *with a wine goblet.*) Have
some champagne, Madame. C'est tres jolie.

SERPUHOVSKY. C'est tres jolie! Drink Mathieu, drink. (*Sings.*)
COUNT THE STARS IN HEAVEN'S VAULT—WHERE
     BEGIN, MY SWEET?
FOR WE'RE DESTINED TO A LIFE SPENT IN SIN,
     MY SWEET
BUT IS THAT SO BAD A STATE TO BE IN, MY SWEET?
GYPSIES.
BUT IS THAT SO BAD A STATE TO BE IN, MY
     SWEET?

(*On the last line the Gypsies start to exit, thinking they are no longer needed when* SERPUHOVSKY *resumes singing, they return.*)

SERPUHOVSKY.
IF GOD FORGIVES THE WICKED
AND CHRIST COULD PARDON JUDAS
ON JUDGMENT DAY THE JUDGE
WILL PITY A PIPSQUEAK LIKE ME!

(MATHIEU, *tiring of the* PRINCE, *eyes the* GYPSY MAN *and slides over to him. She works her hand up his leg. As the surprised* GYPSY *plucks three strong notes,* MATHIEU *plucks his leg like a bass fiddle. He smiles sheepishly.*)

LIVING WITHOUT MATTHEW, WITHOUT LUKE
LIFE GOES BY SO QUICKLY
WHEN THEY CLOSE YOUR EYES WITH SILVER
     COINS
IT'S TOO LATE TO START TO LIVE!
MATHIEU. (*Looking directly at the* GYPSY MAN, *over the* PRINCE.) Bravo! This Russian chanson—charmante!
SERPUHOVSKY. Ah, Mathieu, I'll tell you honestly, I don't like your circus. It's dirty and cold here.
MATHIEU. Sal et froid!
SERPUHOVSKY. But I do love you. When you ride into the center ring, I simply lose all control of myself.
MATHIEU. Ah, mon Prince, morale!
SERPUHOVSKY. (*Sings.*)
GO TO CHURCH AND SAY THE MASS, PRAY'RS
     RECITE, MY SWEET
AND WE'LL CELEBRATE OUR LOVE COME
     TONIGHT, MY SWEET
FOR WHATEVER FEELS ALL RIGHT MUST BE
     RIGHT, MY SWEET

GYPSIES.
FOR WHATEVER FEELS ALL R-I-G-H-T
(SERPUHOVSKY *motions them away.*)
MUST BE RIGHT MY SWEET

(*The couple finally recline with the* PRINCE *over* MATHIEU, *embracing her. The* GYPSIES *collect their pay from* FEOFAN *as they exit.*)

SERPUHOVSKY. Tell me, Mathieu, what would you like? I'll fulfill any wish.

MATHIEU. O-o-o-o-o. (*She quickly sits up leaving the* PRINCE *lying on his stomach.*)

SERPUHOVSKY. Mathieu, I beg you, what is your most secret desire?

MATHIEU, Non, non!

SERPUHOVSKY No? Then I'll tell you your most secret desire. (*He starts to get up, rising to his knees, but* MATHIEU *sits on his back like a circus bareback rider.*)

MATHIEU. S'il vous plait.

SERPUHOVSKY. Do you love the races? (SERPUHOVSKY *looks to* FEOFAN *for help.*)

MATHIEU. Qu'est-ce que sait—the races? (FEOFAN *acts out a horse race. He whistles and cracks an imaginary whip.*)

MATHIEU. The races?

SERPUHOVSKY. Let's go to the races!

MATHIEU. (*Disappointedly.*) The races.

SERPUHOVSKY. To the races!

FEOFAN. To the races! (*The* PRINCE *leads* MATHIEU *off, as she looks back longingly at the oriental rug with its pillows. As the music brightens, members of the* HERD, *who were sitting and watching the scene, remove the boudoir rug and pillows. Others enter in hats, carrying fans, parisols and binoculars. They are transformed into spectators at the races. Couples stroll, circling an imaginary promenade in the center of the racetrack. A boy in a tall hat stands on a high stool in the center taking bets. The* PRINCE *and* MATHIEU *enter. She is wearing a hat, a full skirt variation of her tu-tu and carries a parasol. The* LIEUTENANT, *played by the same actor as* DARLING, *stops to stare flirtatiously at* MATHIEU, *who enjoys the attention.*)

VENDOR. (*Selling refreshments to various customers and calling out his wares repeatedly.*) Champagne, bon-bons, Messieurs et Mesdames! (*The* ANNOUNCER *enters. He is played by the same actor as the* GENERAL *He rings a bell.*)

ANNOUNCER A new race, ladies and gentlemen. The entries are this season's favorites: the trotters Satin, and Little Bull from the Voikoff stables! (*The* CROWD *applauds*) And the winner of four races last week, the trotter Ambrose—from the stables of our eminent English guest, Mr. Willingstone! (*More applause.* MR WILLINGSTONE *bows*)

SERPUHOVSKY. (*To* MATHIEU.) Who do you like?

MATHIEU (*Eyeing the* LIEUTENANT) Satin! J'aime Satin!

SERPUHOVSKY. Satin, the favorite. I can't explain it, Satin is well built, he's in good condition, but he won't win.

LIEUTENANT (*Overhearing the conversation.*) Pardon me, but why not? (*He stares brazenly at* MATHIEU, *who enjoys it.*)

SERPUHOVSKY Why not? He's not in the mood today. As any fool can see, Satin's feeling out of sorts

LIEUTENANT It's not the horse who decides. (*Stares at* MATHIEU) It's the rider who makes the decisions

MATHIEU O-o-o-oh!

SERPUHOVSKY. It's the horse who decides!

CHORUS O-o-o-oh!

LIEUTENANT The rider makes the decisions

SERPUHOVSKY. The horse decides! I'll prove it I'll wager that my patchwork will beat any horse here if they allow him on the track He's not a trotter, but he *is* a thoroughbred

LIEUTENANT. I accept the wager, and I bet a thousand he won't win!

SERPUHOVSKY Done! Feofan!

FEOFAN (*Entering*) Right!

SERPUHOVSKY On to the racetrack, Feofan! I order you and Patchwork to ride the race! And take the curves fast! Fast! Do you hear, Feofan? And if you win it'll be lucky for you too. I'll give you fifty rubles!

FEOFAN Right! (*He goes to* STRIDER *to lead him through the crowd to the track.*)

SERPUHOVSKY. Now Gentlemen, I'll wager a thousand rubles to one that my patchwork, pulling my carriage, with my coachman, will beat any of your favorites! (*The* CROWD *laughs.*) Now's your chance! Gentlemen, place your bets!

ANNOUNCER The pedigreed gelding—what's his name?

SERPUHOVSKY. (*Searching for a name.*) Call him . .
Strider! (*Laughter.*)

ANNOUNCER. Strider! Ladies and Gentlemen, from the stables
of Prince Serpuhovsky, Strider will be placed in the next race by
popular demand! (*He exits.* FEOFAN *takes* STRIDER *off. The
crowd places their bets with the boy. After a moment, the bell
rings, and the sound of running horses is heard. The spectators
watch as if the horses are running around the promenade, which
is in the center of the track. They move from one part of the
promenade to another as they follow the race around the track.
They cheer their favorites.*)

CHORUS MEMBERS.
Come on Satin!
Pull ahead Ambrose!
Easy, pace it!
Look at the English one!
Come on, faster!

(*While the* CROWD *cheers, the* LIEUTENANT *brushes against*
MATHIEU, *kisses her neck and whispers in her ear. The
couple breaks apart quickly as the* PRINCE'S *attention tem-
porarily returns to* MATHIEU.)

SERPUHOVSKY. You'll see, Mathieu! My Feofan is a heavy-
weight; he weighs one hundred and ninety pounds, but I still
believe that my patchwork will win! (*The* PRINCE *becomes in-
volved with the race again as* MATHIEU *returns to the* LIEUTEN-
ANT. *The couple circle "nuzzling"—reminiscent of* DARLING
and VIAZAPURIKHA *in Act One—and exit. The* CROWD *grows
more and more excited following the race. Suddenly a man
shouts out.*)

MAN IN THE CROWD. Look! The patchwork's pulling ahead!

SERPUHOVSKY. Now . . . Strider . . . ! (*A winning bell is
heard.*) He won! (*The entire* CROWD *explodes in an uproar,
jumping up and down excitedly, shouting, throwing hats, etc.*)

FEOFAN. (*Enters with* STRIDER *who has a wreath of red roses
around his neck.*) Watch out! Take care! (SERPUHOVSKY *embraces* STRIDER. *Everyone "freezes" for a moment.*)

STRIDER. That was the happiest day of my life. (*The* CROWD
comes back to life. FEOFAN *continues to walk* STRIDER *to cool
him off. The spectators crowd around the* PRINCE, *rushing over
to him.*)

FIRST MALE SPECTATOR. Your piebald is a wonder! How much do you want for him?

MR. WILLINGSTONE. I say, let me buy him!

FIRST MALE SPECTATOR. One moment, please sir! I can offer you . . .

SECOND MALE SPECTATOR. Bravo Prince! Allow me to congratulate you!

A FEMALE SPECTATOR. Your horse is remarkable! He's taken it all!

THIRD MALE SPECTATOR. Prince, Prince, I can offer you three thousand now, and another three thousand tomorrow . . . before lunch!

FIRST MALE SPECTATOR. Seven thousand. The entire sum . . . right now!

A FEMALE SPECTATOR. Nine thousand, Prince, for your horse!

MR. WILLINGSTONE. I'll give you ten thousand!

THIRD MALE SPECTATOR. Three thousand now and another nine thousand tomorrow . . . after dinner!

MR. WILLINGSTONE. I'm frightfully enthused about your horse, your Highness. I'll give you fifteen thousand. I simply must have that horse!

THE CROWD. Fifteen thousand?!

SERPUHOVSKY. (*He goes over to* STRIDER *and embraces him.*) No, no gentlemen, this isn't a horse, but a friend. I wouldn't part with him for a mountain of gold! Au revoir, gentlemen. Feofan—to the Club! We'll have Gypsies all night long!

ANNOUNCER. (*Enters and crosses to the* PRINCE.) Your Highness! His excellency, the Lieutenant, asked us to forward this to you.

SERPUHOVSKY. The Lieutenant?

ANNOUNCER. His Excellency, the Lieutenant . . .

SERPUHOVSKY. Ah, yes. What is it?

ANNOUNCER. Your winnings, Prince. Please accept these thousand rubles. (*The* CROWD *applauds.*)

SERPUHOVSKY. Gentlemen, I hope that you remember—it's the horse who decides!

ANNOUNCER. Begging your pardon, your Highness. His Excellency, the Lieutenant, has asked me to inform you that it's the *rider* who makes the decisions! (*The* CROWD *titters.*) Will you excuse me, please? (*He exits. Music. The lights grow dimmer.*)

SERPUHOVSKY. (*Noticing her absence.*) Mathieu! Where's Madame Mathieu? (*As several couples drift Offstage, the PRINCE searches among the CROWD asking after MATHIEU. A few members of the CROWD sit, again as horses, to listen to the story.*) Feofan, dear friend, did you notice where Madame Mathieu went? (*FEOFAN shrugs.*)

STRIDER. And following the most joyous event of my life, came my deepest sorrow. He spoke of her as "his." But she had run away with someone else. It was five o'clock, and without even taking me out of harness, he set off after her. (*The PRINCE tears off STRIDER's wreath, throws it Offstage, and stepping into the leather "rope," climbs into the carriage behind FEOFAN.*) I was lashed with a whip, and made to gallop.

SERPUHOVSKY. After them! (*STRIDER removes his harness and holds the wooden cross-piece in his hand. Throughout the chase, he moves the wooden cross-piece of the harness in a circular motion, tracing the movement of a galloping horse. We hear the sound of galloping.*)

FEOFAN. (*Repeatedly cracking his whip on the floor.*) Faster!

SERPUHOVSKY Drive him faster!

FEOFAN. Faster, you devil!

SERPUHOVSKY. Damn it, drive him faster!

FEOFAN Faster! (*They race on, the PRINCE beating on FEOFAN's back.*)

SERPUHOVSKY. There they are!

FEOFAN. Whoa! (*FEOFAN and the PRINCE freeze. The sound of a heartbeat is heard emerging from the fading of STRIDER's galloping hoofbeats.*)

STRIDER. We had gone sixteen miles when we caught up with her and her new lover. I took the Prince back home, but I couldn't stop shivering all night long, and I couldn't eat any thing In the morning, they brought me water and (*Meaningfully.*) I drank it. From then on, I was never again the horse I had been. (*STRIDER hands the harness to FEOFAN who exits one way as the PRINCE exits another. STRIDER watches the PRINCE leave. Meanwhile, the GYPSY WOMAN/HERD MEMBER enters with her guitar.*)

GYPSY WOMAN/HERD MEMBER (*Sings.*)

OH HARD IS LIFE FOR MAN AND HORSE

BUT AS THE YEARS GALLOP BY
YOU'LL VALUE SIMPLE PLEASURES BEST
LIKE GRASS—AND DRINK—AND WARMTH
(*She exits.*)

STRIDER. I got sick They tortured me and maimed me—"doctored" me, as humans call it. My hoofs splintered I had swellings; my legs bent. I had no strength in my chest. Anyone could see I was listless and weak. I was sent to a horse-dealer He fed me on carrots and other things which made me look like the horse I no longer was It was good enough to fool someone who didn't know better, but there was no *strength* in me—no swiftness . . . Whenever there was a customer, the dealer tormented me by coming into my stall and beating me with a great knout—frightening me, driving me into madness. Then he would wipe down the marks on my coat and lead me out. An old woman bought me from the dealer. She was always driving to the Church of St. Nicholas the Miracle Worker and having her coachman flogged. The coachman would come and weep in my stall—it was then I learned that human tears have a pleasant salty taste. Then the old woman died. Her overseer took me into the country and sold me to a peddler, then I was fed on wheat, and got sicker still. I was sold to a peasant. I had to plow, had almost nothing to eat. I cut my leg with a plowshare. I got sicker still. A gypsy traded something for me. He tortured me horribly, and at last I was sold to your overseer. And here I am again. And no one recognized me, except Viazapurikha (STRIDER *slowly goes to the water barrel and takes a long drink before resting his head against the post.*)

MALE HERD MEMBER. (*After a pause in which he has looked at* STRIDER.) Later that evening, the herd came upon their master who had a visitor with him. Both men walked directly into the stable. (*The* HERD *members drift off as the* GROOM *enters, carrying on the same chair from the sale scene in Act One and placing it in the same position. The young* COUNT BOBRINSKY *enters. He is played by the same actor who played* DARLING *and the* LIEUTENANT, *and is dressed in an elaborate dressing robe similar to the one the* PRINCE *wore in Act One.* BOBRINSKY *is about to show the* PRINCE *the horses he has for sale The* PRINCE *enters behind the* COUNT. *He is much older and dulled by alcohol. A servant,* FRITZ, *played by the same actor as* FEOFAN, *enters and remains at attention.*)

I

BOBRINSKY. Take my word for it, Prince, if the Government wants the best for the Imperial stables, *and* is willing to pay for it, you'll find it here. Groom! (*He signals the* GROOM, *who leads out a young mare.*) Here now—nowhere in all Russia will you find a better mare than this!

SERPUHOVSKY. Yes, yes, Bobrinsky. But she's still a bit raw. Too much Dutch blood, that's my opinion.

BOBRINSKY. Look! Just look at those legs! You won't find a better mare for four thousand rubles. Runs like the wind.

SERPUHOVSKY Like the wind?

BOBRINSKY. Like the wind. (*Pause.*) Thirty-five hundred? Fritz, cigars! Bringen sie bitte einen kasten Zo fort!

FRITZ. Ja wohl! (*He exits.*)

SERPUHOVSKY. So how much did Satin cost you?

BOBRINSKY. He cost enough—at least five thousand, maybe six. But Marie liked him, so I bought him for her.

SERPUHOVSKY. Mathieu liked him also . . .

BOBRINSKY. Who?

SERPUHOVSKY. Oh, I was just . . . (FRITZ *enters holding a box of cigars.*)

BOBRINSKY. Have a cigar Prince, you've never smoked any like these.

SERPUHOVSKY. I've smoked everything in my day.

BOBRINSKY. Not these!

SERPUHOVSKY. I prefer my own.

BOBRINSKY. Are yours aged *ten* years?

SERPUHOVSKY. Ten years. Are they really? (*He rustles the dry cigar against his ear, feeling it in his fingers, perhaps snapping it in two, then tosses it back.*) Shall we continue? (BOBRINSKY *cracks his whip and the* GROOM *leads out another horse.*)

BOBRINSKY. This one here I bought from Voikoff.

SERPUHOVSKY. From Voikoff?

BOBRINSKY. Her sire took two prizes: one at Petersburg, one at Moscow. (*The* PRINCE *stares at* STRIDER *who is circling his post.*) Prince?

SERPUHOVSKY. Very nice. Dappled grey. (MARIE *enters. She is played by the same actress who played* VIAZAPURIKHA *and* MATHIEU.)

MARIE. Gentlemen, Prince, tea is being served.

SERPUHOVSKY. (*Going toward her.*) Mathieu . . .

MARIE. (*French pronunciation.*) Pardón?

SERPUHOVSKY. Is that you, Mathieu?

MARIE. I'm afraid I don't understand. (*She moves closer to* BOBRINSKY.)

SERPUHOVSKY. Oh yes . . This is Marie . . Marie . . . (MARIE *shrugs her shoulders, exchanges glances with the* COUNT *before she exits.*)

BOBRINSKY. So, you've started drinking, Prince?

SERPUHOVSKY. What do you mean "started" drinking. I've never *stopped* drinking. I've been drinking all my life. Only recently, drinking has begun to make me drunk. That's something that never happened to me before. It's not due to age. No—I know myself. I'm simply tired of living.

BOBRINSKY Well, life is never easy! (BOBRINSKY *gets ready to show the* PRINCE *another horse.*) Groom!

SERPUHOVSKY. (*His eyes and* STRIDER's *meet.*) How piebald that one is! I had a piebald once, exactly like him. (*The* PRINCE *softly makes the horse sound that he made with* STRIDER *in the first sale scene. He momentarily becomes lost in recollection.*) When I think of what I've lost in my lifetime. I have, dear friend, run through a fortune of over two million rubles. And now, I'm a hundred and twenty thousand in debt. (*He becomes lost again in thought.*)

BOBRINSKY. I believe it. But surely, the reputation for a fortune that size should provide momentum enough to go on living on credit for at least another ten years!

SERPUHOVSKY. It did. But the ten years have expired, the reputation has evaporated, and the momentum is exhausted. (*He approaches* BOBRINSKY *as if getting ready to ask a favor.*) Right now I'd be happy to get my hands on just a thousand rubles and count myself lucky to get away from everyone. I can't stand Moscow anymore. (BOBRINSKY *doesn't react.*) Ah! But why talk about it? What's the use? (SERPUHOVSKY *becomes lost in a dream.* BOBRINSKY's *watch begins musically to chime When he takes it from his pocket, we see it's the same one as the* PRINCE's *in Act One. The* PRINCE *momentarily recognizes the watch.*)

BOBRINSKY. It's getting late, Prince. Let's look at some more horses shall we? I wanted to tell you that in my stud . . .

SERPUHOVSKY. (*Interrupting.*) In your stud . . . there was a time when I loved life and knew how to live it too! Now you talk about racing—you tell me, which is your fastest horse?

Well? Tell me! (BOBRINSKY *indicates to the* GROOM *to bring out another horse.*) Never mind, never mind! The trouble with you horse-breeders is that you do it only for ostentation, not for pleasure, for life! (BOBRINSKY, *disgusted, sits in the chair.*) I was telling you a while ago that I once had a trotter, a well-bred piebald gelding. Something like this poor wreck . . . Oh, what a horse he was! I never had, and you never had, and never will have such a horse I liked him. I never knew a better horse for gait, for speed or strength, or beauty. You were a lad then. You could not have known, but you may have heard, I suppose. All Moscow knew him.

BOBRINSKY. Yes, I think I heard about him. But I was going to tell you that . . .

SERPUHOVSKY. So you heard of him. I bought him just as he was, without pedigree, without proof. But then I knew Voikoff, and I traced him. He was sired by Amiable-the-First And his name . . . (*Striving to remember*) Strider! That was his name, Strider. Because he had a stride like the measure of cloth—this long! He resembled this poor thing There aren't horses like him anymore, dear friend. Ah! What a time that was. (*Sings to himself.*)

LIVING WITHOUT MATTHEW—WITHOUT LUKE
LIFE GOES BY SO QUICKLY . . .

Eh! That was a golden time! I was twenty-five. I had eighty thousand a year, not a single gray hair, all my teeth, and every one of them a pearl. Whatever I touched, prospered. And yet, it all came to an end . . . (*Sings to himself.*)

WHEN THEY CLOSE YOUR EYES WITH SILVER
    COINS
IT'S TOO LATE TO START TO LIVE!

(*He collapses at* BOBRINSKY's *feet.*)

BOBRINSKY. Fritz. (BOBRINSKY *motions to* FRITZ *to help the* PRINCE *up as he steps over the fallen man.*)

FRITZ. (*Approaching* SERPUHOVSKY.) Mein liever Herr, bitte!

SERPUHOVSKY. Feofan?

FRITZ. Feofan?

SERPUHOVSKY. Have some champagne, madame. C'est tres jolie!

BOBRINSKY. Who's Feofan? This is my servant Fritz.

SERPUHOVSKY. Fritz? Ah, what a coachman I had—Feofan

was his name. He was a splendid fellow. I liked him. But he also drank himself to death!

MARIE. (*Entering.*) Gentleman! Prince, I beg you, tea is served! (*Goes to* BOBRINSKY. *They move out of earshot of the* PRINCE.) He's unbearable.

BOBRINSKY. He's drunk, and lies faster than he can talk.

MARIE. Why do you put up with him?

BOBRINSKY. His relatives got him this job buying horses for the government—so I *have* to put up with him!

MARIE. He tried to flirt with me.

BOBRINSKY. He tried to ask *me* for a loan.

MARIE. No! (*As they exit.*)

MARIE and BOBRINSKY. We're waiting, Prince. (*They exit.*)

FRITZ. (*Trying to help the* PRINCE *up.*) Bitte.

SERPUHOVSKY. I must have told a lot of lies. But he's an awful swine. Cheap—like a merchant! But I'm an awful swine myself. I used to keep others, now others keep me. (*He breaks away and leans on the chair.*) Phoo! It's really amazing how much this poor wreck resembles Strider. (*The* PRINCE *walks slowly over to* STRIDER. STRIDER *places his head on the* PRINCE's *shoulder. For an instant, the* PRINCE *responds as if he remembers. He begins to touch* STRIDER *as if to pet him, but is repelled by the mangy horse. He pulls away.*) No . . . no . . . (*He starts to slowly cross away, looks back once more.* STRIDER *leans toward him, staring at him, straining on the rope.*) No . . . no! (*He turns away and collapses onto* FRITZ *who leads him off.*)

STRIDER. And so he never recognized me. Well—how could he? (*Music. Several members of the* HERD *enter and address the audience and* STRIDER.)

MALE HERD MEMBER. There is a majestic old age . . .

ANOTHER MALE HERD MEMBER. (*The* GENERAL.) There is a repulsive old age . . .

FEMALE HERD MEMBER. There is a pitiful old age . . .

ANOTHER FEMALE HERD MEMBER. There is also an old age that is both majestic and repulsive. (*Music. The* CHORUS *disperses. A* MALE HERD MEMBER *takes away the chair.* STRIDER *stands alone.*)

STRIDER. (*Itches himself.*) Something itches me terribly. Something itches me terribly. (*Scratches himself against the post. The barn door bangs open as at the beginning of the play, and we see a shaft of light* COUNT BOBRINSKY *enters singing a tune to himself. He leads a horse from a stall and begins to harness it.)*

BOBRINSKY. (*Sings.*)
OH NEVER HAVE I THIRSTED FOR LIFE SO MUCH
BUT NOW THE HOUR HAS COME
AND NOW I MUST DIE . . .
(BOBRINSKY *goes to* STRIDER, *touches him, noticing his skin.*)
Damn! Vaska!

STRIDER. It itches me terribly.

BOBRINSKY. What?

STRIDER. Itches. (VASKA *snores.*)

BOBRINSKY. Vaska! Are you asleep?

VASKA. Huh? What? No, I'm just . . .

BOBRINSKY. Look at him! (*Cracking his whip.*) *Look* at him!

VASKA. (*Goes to* STRIDER, *feels his stomach and looks into his mouth.*) It's the mange, your Excellency. Let me sell him to the gypsies.

BOBRINSKY. The gypsies? What's the use? Cut his throat.

VASKA. Cut his throat. We'll do that.

BOBRINSKY. Only get it done today. (*Exits singing "Oh never . . . "*)

VASKA. Cut his throat. So that's how it is, eh? . . . (*Swings at* STRIDER) Now you're going to get it. (*He goes to the grindstone to sharpen his knife as in Act One. Music. The* GROOM *enters, and he and* VASKA *exchange glances. The* GROOM *goes and unhitches* STRIDER. *Stroking the horse to comfort him, he leads* STRIDER *to Center Stage.* VASKA *joins them.*)

VASKA A fine horse, in his day.

GROOM. A fine hide too. If he'd been better fed. (*The* GROOM *draws back* STRIDER'S *head.*)

STRIDER. They're going to "doctor" me. Well—let them— (*As* VASKA *draws his knife across* STRIDER'S *throat, we hear the shimmering sound of Indian bell chimes. The stage is suddenly bathed in blue light. The* GROOM *and* VASKA *exit.* STRIDER'S DEATH We hear the approaching sound of a galloping horse. A blurred composite of several bits of previous pantomimes.* STRIDER'S *birth, his victory at the races, etc. As the roaring of the crowd fades into the receding sound of his galloping,* STRIDER *slowly collapses, retracing his wobbly attempts to walk and roll on the floor. Music. The* FEMALE HERD MEMBER *with* *the butterfly enters.* STRIDER *attempts to bite at it. It alights on his outstretched hand as he dies. The lights suddenly come up. The entire company enters. The Actor playing* SERPUHOVSKY *is wiping his make-up with the towel* STRIDER *used in Act One. The Actor playing* STRIDER *sits up.*)

MALE CHORUS MEMBER. At the end of the week, there lay behind the brick barn only the great skull and two shoulder blades. (*After mopping his own brow,* SERPUHOVSKY *tosses* STRIDER *the make-up towel to remove his piebald face make-up.*)

FEMALE CHORUS MEMBER. All the rest had been dragged away by the dogs and the wolves.

STRIDER. In the summer, a peasant collecting bones carried off the skull and shoulder blades, and put them to use.

MALE CHORUS MEMBER The dead body of Prince Serpuhovsky, which still walked about the earth, eating and drinking, was buried long after.

FEMALE CHORUS MEMBER. It had long been useless to everyone. It had only been a burden.

SERPUHOVSKY. (*Finishing the removal of his moustache and side-burns.*) But still, the dead who bury the dead found it necessary to stuff this already decaying, swollen body into a fine uniform, into fine boots; and place it in a fine new coffin, with new tassels on the four corners. Neither the skin, nor the flesh, nor the bones were of any use to any one.

THE ENTIRE COMPANY. Neither the skin, nor the flesh, nor the bones were of any use to any one. (*They gradually "transform" into their horse characterizations as the lights fade, silhouetting the actors against the sky.*)

THE END

POST PRODUCTION NOTE

The song "Live Long Enough" was not part of either the original Leningrad or Chelsea Theater Center productions of STRIDER. It was inserted into the Broadway production after it had opened and had been playing at the Helen Hayes Theater for several months.

Sung by Strider tied to his post, it was placed after his line in the second act, "And so he never recognized me. Well—how could he?" The music cue for the Chorus' entrance, resuming the stage action, followed the song as Strider returned to his post. The song was accompanied by an offstage chorus.

LIVE LONG ENOUGH

LIVE LONG ENOUGH
LIVE LONG ENOUGH
LIVE LONG ENOUGH
AND YOU'LL COME TO LEARN
THE SORROWS AND THE JOYS
ARE THE SAME, THEY'RE THE SAME

LIVE LONG ENOUGH
LIVE LONG ENOUGH
PLEASURES AND PAINS
COME SIDE BY SIDE
THE HEARTACHES WITH THE HOPES
HAND IN HAND, INTERTWINED

SORROW AND JOY ARE ONE
JUST LIKE THE MOON AND SUN
ONE FOR THE DAY IS BRIGHT
SOFTER IS ONE FOR NIGHT
BOTH ARE THE WONDER OF LIGHT

WHY ALL THIS SHOULD HAPPEN
IT'S BEYOND ME, BEYOND ME TO SAY
I KNOW THAT IT HAPPENS
IT HAPPENS EXACTLY THIS WAY

LIVE LONG ENOUGH
LIVE LONG ENOUGH
YOU'LL LEARN TO LOVE
BOTH LAUGHTER AND TEARS
THE LAUGHTER AND TEARS
THAT HAVE COME WITH THE YEARS

LIVE LONG ENOUGH
LIVE LONG ENOUGH
LIVE LONG ENOUGH
AND YOU'LL COME TO SEE
HOW LAUGHTER CAN BE SAD
AND HOW SWEET WOE CAN BE

SORROW AND JOY ARE ONE
WE MUST HAVE BOTH, OR NONE
BOTH HAVE THE POWER TO HEAL
BOTH TEACH THE HEART WHAT IS REAL
THEY SHOW US TO LIVE IS TO FEEL
LIVE LONG ENOUGH
LIVE LONG ENOUGH
LIVE LONG ENOUGH

TREASURE ISLAND
Ken Ludwig

All Groups / Adventure / 10m, 1f (doubling) / Areas

Based on the masterful adventure novel by Robert Louis Stevenson, *Treasure Island* is a stunning yarn of piracy on the tropical seas. It begins at an inn on the Devon coast of England in 1775 and quickly becomes an unforgettable tale of treachery and mayhem featuring a host of legendary swashbucklers including the dangerous Billy Bones (played unforgettably in the movies by Lionel Barrymore), the sinister two-timing Israel Hands, the brassy woman pirate Anne Bonney, and the hideous form of evil incarnate, Blind Pew. At the center of it all are Jim Hawkins, a 14-year-old boy who longs for adventure, and the infamous Long John Silver, who is a complex study of good and evil, perhaps the most famous hero-villain of all time. Silver is an unscrupulous buccaneer-rogue whose greedy quest for gold, coupled with his affection for Jim, cannot help but win the heart of every soul who has ever longed for romance, treasure and adventure.

THE SCENE
Theresa Rebeck

Little Theatre / Drama / 2m, 2f / Interior Unit Set
A young social climber leads an actor into an extra-marital affair, from which he then creates a full-on downward spiral into alcoholism and bummery. His wife runs off with his best friend, his girlfriend leaves, and he's left with… nothing.

"Ms. Rebeck's dark-hued morality tale contains enough fresh insights into the cultural landscape to freshen what is essentially a classic boy-meets-bad-girl story."
- New York Times

"Rebeck's wickedly scathing observations about the sort of self-obsessed New Yorkers who pursue their own interests at the cost of their morality and loyalty."
- New York Post

"The Scene is utterly delightful in its comedic performances, and its slowly unraveling plot is thought-provoking and gut-wrenching."
- Show Business Weekly

THE MUSICAL OF MUSICALS (THE MUSICAL!)
Music by Eric Rockwell
Lyrics by Joanne Bogart
Book by Eric Rockwell and Joanne Bogart

2m, 2f / Musical / Unit Set
The Musical of Musicals (The Musical!) is a musical about musicals! In this hilarious satire of musical theatre, one story becomes five delightful musicals, each written in the distinctive style of a different master of the form, from Rodgers and Hammerstein to Stephen Sondheim. The basic plot: June is an ingenue who can't pay the rent and is threatened by her evil landlord. Will the handsome leading man come to the rescue? The variations are: a Rodgers & Hammerstein version, set in Kansas in August, complete with a dream ballet; a Sondheim version, featuring the landlord as a tortured artistic genius who slashes the throats of his tenants in revenge for not appreciating his work; a Jerry Herman version, as a splashy star vehicle; an Andrew Lloyd Webber version, a rock musical with themes borrowed from Puccini; and a Kander & Ebb version, set in a speakeasy in Chicago. This comic valentine to musical theatre was the longest running show in the York Theatre Company's 35-year history before moving to Off-Broadway.

"Witty! Refreshing! Juicily! Merciless!"
- Michael Feingold, *Village Voice*

"A GIFT FROM THE MUSICAL THEATRE GODS!"
– *TalkinBroadway.com*

"Real Wit, Real Charm! Two Smart Writers and Four Winning Performers! You get the picture, it's GREAT FUN!"
- *The New York Times*

"Funny, charming and refreshing!
It hits its targets with sophisticated affection!"
- *New York Magazine*

SAMUELFRENCH.COM